EASY   Weeks, Sarah.
Wee   Overboard!

WITHDRAWN
Woodridge Public Library

MAR 1 9 2007	JUN 0 8 2007
APR 1 9 2007	JUN 2 1 2007
	JUL 0 6 2007
MAY 0 7 2007	JUL 1 7 2007
	OCT 1 2 2007
MAY 2 4 2007	
MAY 3 0 2007	AUG 0 4 2008

WOODRIDGE PUBLIC LIBRARY
3 PLAZA DRIVE
WOODRIDGE, IL 60517-5014
(630) 964-7899

P9-CDT-544

Over

By

Sarah Weeks

Illustrated by

Sam Williams

board!

Harcourt, Inc.

Orlando   Austin   New York
San Diego   Toronto   London

WOODRIDGE PUBLIC LIBRARY
3 PLAZA DRIVE
WOODRIDGE, IL 60517-5014
(630) 964-7899

Text copyright © 2006 by Sarah Weeks
Illustrations copyright © 2006 by Sam Williams Limited

All rights reserved. No part of this publication may be reproduced or transmitted in
any form or by any means, electronic or mechanical, including photocopy, recording, or any
information storage and retrieval system, without permission in writing from the publisher.

Requests for permission to make copies of any part of the work should be mailed to the following address:
Permissions Department, Harcourt, Inc., 6277 Sea Harbor Drive, Orlando, Florida 32887-6777.

www.HarcourtBooks.com

Library of Congress Cataloging-in-Publication Data
Weeks, Sarah.
Overboard!/Sarah Weeks; illustrated by Sam Williams.
p.   cm.
Summary: From morning to night, a young child playfully grabs and
throws items, including a bathtime rubber ducky and snacktime raisins.
[1. Play—Fiction.   2. Toddlers—Fiction.   3. Stories in rhyme.]
I. Williams, Sam, 1955– ill.   II. Title.
PZ8.3.W4215Ov   2006
[E]—dc22   2004023344
ISBN-13: 978-0152-05046-7   ISBN-10: 0-15-205046-9

First edition
A C E G H F D B

The illustrations in this book were done in
charcoal, pastel, and watercolor on hot-press paper.
The display type was set in OptiBernhardGothic.
The text type was set in Sassoon Sans.
Color separations by Bright Arts Ltd., Hong Kong
Printed and bound by Tien Wah Press, Singapore
This book was printed on totally chlorine-free Stora Enso Matte paper.
Production supervision by Pascha Gerlinger
Designed by April Ward

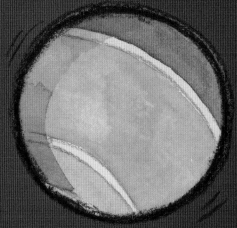

To Ian Patrick Evans
—S.W.

For Andrew—
the kid who *always*
goes overboard!
—S.W.

Drippy, slippy-slidey peaches.
Peachy peaches, nice and fat.
Peaches going . . .

overboard!
Peaches, peaches,

Squeaky, leaky rubber ducky.

Lucky ducky time to fly.

Rubber ducky . . .

overboard!

Rubber ducky,

bye,

bye,

bye!

Favorite jammies...

Little lambies...

overboard!

Bunny wipers...

overboard!

Bunny diapers...

overboard!

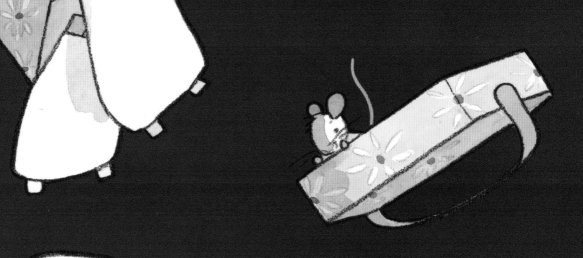
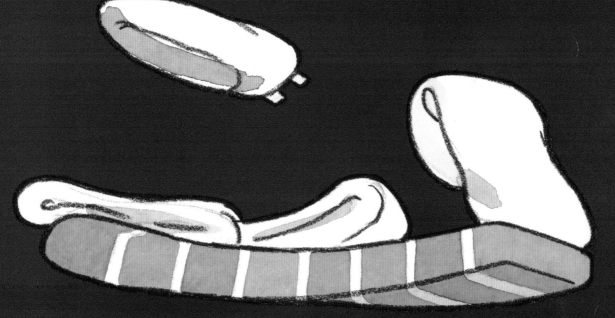

Sprinkly, crinkly row of raisins.
Wrinkly raisins, whatcha think?
Raisins going . . .

overboard!

Crinkly raisins,

Plink!

Plink!

Plink!

Oh no!

Overboard!

Heave-
ho!

Bunny thinks it's time to try
overboard from way up high.

Bunny overboard?

Oh my!

Good thing Mama's right close by.

Nippy-nappy sleepy one,
didn't we have lots of fun?

Now it's time to tuck in tight.
Time to kiss and say good night.

Close the window.
Pull the cord.
Time for one last...

overboard!